D0342008

Welcome to
Hopscotch Hill School!
In Miss Sparks's class,
you will make friends
with children just like you.
They love school,
and they love to learn!
Keep an eye out for Razzi,
the class pet rabbit.
He may be anywhere!
See if you can spot him
as you read the story.

Welcome!

Miss Sparks

Lindy

Hallie

Logan

Gwen

Avery

Spencer

Nathan

Razzi

Skylar

Delaney

Connor

Published by Pleasant Company Publications
Copyright © 2005 by American Girl, LLC
All rights reserved. No part of this book may be used or reproduced
in any manner whatsoever without written permission except in the case
of brief quotations embodied in critical articles and reviews.
For information, address:
Book Editor, Pleasant Company Publications, 8400 Fairway Place,
P.O. Box 620998, Middleton, WI 53562.

Visit our Web site at **americangirl.com**.

Printed in China
05 06 07 08 09 10 C&C 10 9 8 7 6 5 4 3 2

Hopscotch Hill School™ and logo, Hopscotch Hill™,
Where a love for learning grows™, and American Girl®
are trademarks of American Girl, LLC.

Cataloging-in-Publication data available from the Library of Congress

American Girl®

Lindy's
Happy Ending

by Valerie Tripp illustrated by Joy Allen

Lindy's Nest

Lindy grinned.

She could tell that Miss Sparks

had good news.

The sparkles on her eyeglasses

were glittering.

"Boys and girls," said Miss Sparks.

"We will have a visitor today.

Ranger Bell is coming.

She is bringing duck eggs

for us to hatch."

The children cheered, "Hurray!"

Miss Sparks said, "We will take

very good care of the eggs.

We will make sure that

they stay safe and warm.

In 28 days

the eggs will hatch.

Then we will

have ducklings."

"Ducklings!" the children cheered.

Miss Sparks said, "The ducklings will

live in a box in our nature corner.

We will feed them and watch them grow.

Ranger Bell will come back

when they are big.

She will take them to the Nature Center.

That is where they will live."

Lindy's Nest

Lindy had a great idea.

She raised her hand.

She said, "Let's fix up our

nature corner for the ducklings.

Let's get some big rocks and a tree stump.

We could get some hay

and spread it around, and—"

Miss Sparks said, "Whoa, Lindy!

Let's stop and think.

It's a good idea to

make space for the eggs.

And let's clean up our classroom.

Then we will be ready for our visitor."

Lindy and all the other children

liked Miss Sparks's ideas.

Miss Sparks helped

the children make

 a list of jobs.

Jobs to Do
1. Dust the bookshelves.
2. Sweep the floor.
3. Wash the cupboards.
4. Straighten the desks and chairs.

Lindy and Avery had the job

of dusting the bookshelves.

Lindy rushed to the bookshelves.

She said, "Let's pull ALL the books

off EVERY shelf."

Avery asked, "Won't that be extra work?"

"Oh, no," said Lindy.

"It will be extra fun."

Lindy and Avery pulled ALL the books

off EVERY shelf.

Thump, bump! It was fun!

Lindy's Happy Ending

Lindy got off to a great start.

She dusted some shelves.

She put some books back.

Then Lindy sighed.

Putting the books back on the shelf

was not as much fun

as pulling them off had been.

Lindy looked at the books around her.

They looked like a nest.

"Look at me, Avery," Lindy said.

"I'm a duckling in a nest."

"Your nest is cute!" said Avery.

Lindy added more books to her nest.

Spencer walked by.

"Quack, quack," said Lindy.

"I'm a duckling in a nest."

Spencer laughed.

He quacked too.

Then it was time for lunch.

Lindy waddled off

with Spencer.

"Wait!" said Avery.

"We are not finished."

But Lindy was

already gone.

Avery had to put the books back

on the shelf all by herself.

After lunch Ranger Bell came.

She brought the eggs in an incubator.

She said, "This room looks great!

I think that your class

will take good care of

the eggs and the ducklings."

"We will!" promised the children.

The sparkles on

Miss Sparks's eyeglasses glittered.

"Class," she said, "I have an idea.

Ranger Bell will come back to get

the ducklings when they are big.

She will decide if we have

taken good care of them.

If we have, we will all go

to the Nature Center someday

to visit our ducks.

It will be a field trip."

"A field trip!" cheered the children.

Lindy said, "We will do a good job!

We will take great care

of the eggs AND the ducklings.

We'll do the best job ever in the world!"

Lindy's Ducky Ideas

The eggs were cozy in the incubator.

The children loved to look at them.

Every day Lindy counted the eggs:

1, 2, 3, 4, 5, 6, 7, 8, 9, 10.

Miss Sparks wrote some

math problems on the board.

All the problems were

about eggs and ducklings.

Gwen was Lindy's math partner.

Lindy had a great idea.

She said, "Let's draw our answers."

Gwen asked, "Won't that be extra work?"

"Oh, no," said Lindy.

"It will be extra fun."

Lindy got off to a great start.

She read the first problem.

"4 ducklings plus 4 ducklings," she said.

"That equals 8 ducklings."

Lindy drew 8 cute little ducklings.

Scritch, scratch!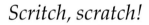

It was fun!

Gwen read the second problem.

"5 eggs plus 5 eggs," she said.

"That equals 10 eggs."

Lindy drew 1, 2, 3, 4 eggs.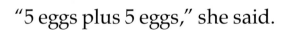

Then Lindy sighed.

10 eggs was a lot.

Drawing eggs was not as much fun

as drawing ducklings.

Lindy took out her crayons.

She colored in the ducklings.

Delaney came by.

She said, "Those ducklings are so cute!

Can you show me how to draw them?"

Lindy said, "Sure!"

Lindy went off with Delaney.

"Wait!" said Gwen. "We are not finished."

But Lindy was already gone.

Gwen had to finish the

math problems all by herself.

Later Miss Sparks read a book

about ducks to the class.

Then Miss Sparks gave

the children an activity sheet.

They had to number pictures

to tell what happened first,

next, and last in the book.

Hallie was Lindy's partner.

Lindy had a great idea.

She said, "Let's cut out the pictures

and glue them in the right order."

Hallie asked, "Won't that be extra work?"

"Oh, no," said Lindy.

"It will be extra fun."

Lindy got off to a great start.

She and Hallie numbered

the pictures 1, 2, 3.

Then Lindy cut the pictures out.

Snip! Clip! It was fun!

She glued the first picture in place.

Some of the glue got on her fingers.

Lindy sighed.

Gluing the pictures in place

was not as much fun

as cutting them out.

It was messy and boring.

Lindy saw that Hallie was gluing

the second picture in place.

Lindy said, "I'm going to

wash the glue off my fingers."

"Wait!" said Hallie.

"We are not finished."

But Lindy was already gone.

Hallie had to finish the activity sheet

all by herself.

Gwen and Avery stopped by.

Avery said, "We know how
you feel, Hallie."

"Yes," said Gwen.

"Lindy has great ideas, but—"

All three girls said together,

"She doesn't finish what she starts!"

At last the eggs hatched!

All the children were delighted.

The ducklings were very cute.

They were little balls of fluff.

"Peep, peep," they cheeped.

The children took turns

cleaning out the ducklings' box.

They gave the ducklings

water and food.

The ducklings grew fast.

In a few weeks

they were teenage ducks.

"Quack, quack!" they quacked.

Miss Sparks said, "Boys and girls!

Always remember to put

the lid back on the ducks' box.

The ducks are big enough to get out."

The children said, "We will remember."

After a few more weeks

Miss Sparks said, "Boys and girls!

The ducks are almost grown up.

Ranger Bell is coming to get them

tomorrow morning."

Lindy had a great idea.

She said, "Let's clean up our room.

Ranger Bell will be pleased.

Then we can go on the field trip."

"Yes!" said all the children.

Everyone worked hard

to make the room look extra nice.

During recess Lindy and Nathan

stayed inside to take care of the ducks.

Nathan took the dirty newspaper

out of the ducks' box.

Miss Sparks said, "Nathan,

let's put that outside in the dumpster."

Nathan and Miss Sparks left.

Lindy put clean newspaper

in the ducks' box.

She gave the ducks water and food.

Lindy sighed.

The jobs were too simple and easy!

Then Lindy had a great idea.

She would wash the water bowl!

Lindy lifted the lid of the box

and took out the water bowl.

She filled the sink with soapy water.

She swooshed the bowl in it.

Splish, splash! It was fun!

Just then Lindy heard

Miss Sparks shout,

"OH NO!"

Lindy turned around.

The ducks were

out of their box!

Duck Disaster

Quack, quack!" the ducks quacked.

"Catch them!" said Miss Sparks.

Lindy, Nathan, and Miss Sparks

chased the ducks all over the room.

The ducks were fast!

They hopped up on chairs.

They scooted under desks.

They hid behind bookshelves.

"Quack, quack!" they quacked.

Lindy's Happy Ending

Lindy, Nathan, and Miss Sparks

caught the ducks one by one.

At last all the ducks were back

in their box.

Just then the rest of the class

came back from recess.

They could not believe their eyes.

Oh, what a mess the room was!

Papers were all over the floor.

Chairs were knocked every which way.

Duck Disaster

Desks were tipped over and
their insides spilled out.
Feathers floated in the air.
There was duck poop everywhere.
The sparkles on Miss Sparks's
eyeglasses were not glittering at all.
The children were very sad.
Spencer said, "Now Ranger Bell
won't be pleased.
Now we will never go on the field trip."

Lindy said, "I am so sorry!

I did not put the top back

on the ducks' box.

This mess is all my fault.

So I will clean it all up right now.

Then our room will look great

when Ranger Bell comes

tomorrow morning."

Lindy rushed to get the mop.

Miss Sparks said, "Whoa, Lindy!

You can't clean this up

all by yourself."

Hallie said, "Let's ALL help Lindy."

"Yes," said Gwen.

"We'll be a clean-up team."

"Okay!" said the rest of the class.

Avery said, "Lindy, you can be

the captain of our clean-up team.

I will be your first helper.

Before we begin

let's stop and think.

What is the best way to do this job?"

Lindy thought.

She said, "Let's make a list of

everything that needs to be done."

Miss Sparks and the children

made a list of jobs.

Miss Sparks helped the children

choose their jobs.

Lindy and Gwen chose to

clean up the poop

and feathers.

Gwen said, "Lindy,

I will be your next helper.

I will help you stick

with the job you started."

"Okay," said Lindy.

Gwen and Lindy worked hard.

After a while Lindy sighed.

She said, "There are so

many feathers and so much poop!"

Jobs to Do
1. Pick up papers.
2. Put the desks back.
3. Put the chairs back.
4. Clean up poop and feathers.

Gwen said, "Yes. But don't give up.

Look at all that

you have already done."

Gwen helped Lindy keep on cleaning

until all the feathers

and poop were gone.

Hallie said, "Lindy, I will be

your last helper.

I will help you check the list.

We will make sure that all the jobs

are completely done."

Hallie and Lindy looked

at the list of jobs.

They put a check next to

every job that

was completely done.

The next morning

Ranger Bell came to get the ducks.

She said, "This room looks great.

The ducks look great too.

Miss Sparks, I think the children

have earned a field trip. Do you?"

All the children looked at Miss Sparks.

The sparkles on her eyeglasses glittered.

Miss Sparks said, "Yes!"

"Hurray!" cheered the children.

Everyone had a wonderful

time on the field trip.

Lindy smiled at her friends.

"Thank you," she said.

"You showed me that doing a good job

from start to finish

is the way to a happy ending.

Dear Parents . . .

I s your child like Lindy: great at hatching ducky ideas but sometimes a little flighty about following them through to the finish? Children usually start new projects with enthusiasm, energy, and lots of creative ideas for making things more fun. But sometimes their great ideas get too big, and children are overwhelmed by the responsibility they've taken on. Sometimes they run out of steam, lose interest, or simply forget to finish what they've started. And sometimes they fly off because they are distracted by their *next* big idea.

How can you help your child remember to be responsible and to stick with a task from the beginning through the middle to the end? Try some of the following activities, suggested by the Hopscotch Hill School advisory board, to inspire your child to start smart, help her stay motivated in the middle, and cheer her on to a fabulous finish.

The Beginning

What do all happy endings have in common? A good beginning. So give your child a head start by reminding her to use her head *before* she starts a project. Help her keep the job child-sized, divide the whole into doable parts, and choose the best way to proceed.

- Read *Lindy's Happy Ending* aloud with your child. Ask her to stop you by holding up her hand like a traffic cop each time Lindy has another "great idea" that makes her task grow too big or too complicated to complete. Talk about ways that Lindy could have made her tasks extra fun without letting them get out of hand. Next time your child's plans sound too grand, **use the "stop" hand** gesture. Then point to your head and say, "Think!" Add a wink so that she'll know you have confidence in her ability to handily handle tasks and responsibilities that are the right size for her.

- Help your child divide giant jobs into doable steps by making a **staircase "to do" list**. Ask her to draw a staircase of four or five steps and label the top step with the name or a picture of the task, such as "clean my bedroom." Then help her label the bottom step with what she needs to do first, the second step with what she needs to do next, and so on. Put the list where your child can see it while she works, and let her stick a sticker on each step she completes on her way to the top.

- When your child pulls out her art supplies to make a gift or drawing or to decorate a thank-you note, join in the fun by providing her with creative materials like macaroni, buttons, scraps of cloth, or dried flowers. Brainstorm all the different ways in which she could proceed with her project, and then help her **choose which way is best,** given the amount of time and the materials she has. Remind her that planning takes time—and clean-up responsibilities do, too.

The Middle

Even if your child gets all her ducks in a row and starts off strong, she might get bogged down in the middle of a job. Sometimes the end looks a long way off, the responsibility looks too big, and it's hard for your child not to get discouraged, distracted, or bored. How can you meet her in the middle and help her stay enthusiastic and interested all the way to the other side?

• **Jazz it up!** Let your child choose her favorite CD or tape and see if music inspires her to keep working. At the end of each song, she can decide to rest and relax through the next number—or rock 'n' roll on until the job is done.

- Break it up! Plan ahead for fun breaks by marking natural stopping points. Put a bookmark at the end of a chapter, for example, or set the oven timer to go off after 15 minutes. When your child gets to the breaking point, encourage her to refresh herself with a snack or ten jumping jacks before she continues her task. If her attention span has been stretched to its limit, let her stop and **"push the pause button."** She'll probably be ready to get going again after five minutes or so.

- Change it up! When your child's winding down, encourage her to **switch gears.** If she has been absorbed in a quiet, sitting-down sort of task, encourage her to try finishing the job while standing up and bouncing on her toes, or doing the job double-time. If she has been rushing, suggest that she try moving in slow motion and as silently as possible. Trying a new way will renew her as she's on her way to completing her task.

Jobs to Do
1. Pick up papers.
2. Put the desks back.
3. Put the chairs back.
4. Clean up poop and
   feathers.

The End

The home stretch can be the longest, toughest stretch of all. It's often hard to keep your child focused when she's so close to finishing. You may need to gently remind her to be responsible all the way to the end and show her that for a job to be "all done," it must also be "well done."

• Sing a song or recite a rhyme, but stop before the final line and let your child supply it. **Have a goofy brainstorm** with her to come up with funny consequences of things left half-done, such as wearing only one shoe, brushing the hair on only one side of her head, or stopping in a race before crossing the finish line. Talk about how, just like a song or poem or race, a responsibility is not over until a job is 100 percent finished.

Dear Parents . . .

- Next time you make a grocery list, ask your child to draw a little box by the name of each item. As you shop, let her **put a check in each box** as you put that item into your cart. Checking off jobs on a "to do" list is fun to do, too. You will be showing your child how to double-check to be sure a job is truly completed.

- If all's well that ends well, then the last step in any project or task is to be sure the task has been well done. Your child may find it fun to pretend that she's a bird flying over—and spying over—the project she's just completed. Giving a job one last going-over from a **bird's-eye view** will help her make sure that she hasn't overlooked or forgotten anything.

- When you reward and reinforce your child for completing a job responsibly, **choose a reward that fits**. Just as Lindy's reward for cleaning up after the ducklings was a field trip to the Nature Center, your child's reward for cleaning her bedroom might be a pretty potted plant or a new picture frame. Be sure to tell her how proud you are to have a child who knows that doing a job from start to finish is the way to a happy ending.

This story and the "Dear Parents" activities were developed with guidance from the Hopscotch Hill School advisory board:

Dominic Gullo is a professor of Early Childhood Education at Queens College, City University of New York. He is a member of the governing board of the National Association for the Education of Young Children, and he is a consultant to school districts across the country in the areas of early childhood education, curriculum, and assessment.

Margaret Jensen has taught beginning reading for 32 years and is currently a math resource teacher in the Madison Metropolitan School District, Wisconsin. She has served on committees for the International Reading Association and the Wisconsin State Reading Association, and has been president of the Madison Area Reading Council. She has presented at workshops and conferences in the areas of reading, writing, and children's literature.

Kim Miller is a school psychologist at Stephens Elementary in Madison, Wisconsin, where she works with children, parents, and teachers to help solve—and prevent—problems related to learning and adjustment to the classroom setting.

Virginia Pickerell has worked with teachers and parents as an educational consultant and counselor within the Madison Metropolitan School District. She has researched and presented workshops on topics such as learning processes, problem solving, and creativity. She is also a former director of Head Start.